GW00382141

Secret Summer

Elizabeth Grey

Please visit www.elizabeth-grey.com **to sign up to Elizabeth Grey's newsletter and for more information on her books.**

Facebook: www.facebook.com/elizabethgreyauthor
Twitter: www.twitter.com/elizabethjgrey
Instagram: www.instagram.com/elizabethgreyauthor

Secret Summer - The Agency #1.5

Published 2018
ISBN: 9781720172376

Set in 12 pt, Times New Roman.

Cover designed by Elizabeth Grey Art & Illustration of South Shields, Tyne and Wear, UK.

Copy Edited by Kia Thomas Editing of South Shields, Tyne and Wear, UK. www.kiathomasediting.com
www.twitter.com/kiathomasedits

DEDICATION

For Chris,

We’ll always have Santorini.

SIGN UP TO MY MAILING LIST

www.elizabeth-grey.com/mailing-list

To receive pre-launch previews, news, special offers and much more!

1

"CLOSE YOUR EYES. NO PEEKING."

I reluctantly do as I'm told. I take hold of Ethan's hand and hear him unlock the door to his apartment. "Ethan, you know I hate surprises, right?" He sighs. I can picture his face: cocky expression, eye roll, trademark grin. "I swear if there's something horrific like a vat of slime waiting for me at the end of this adventure, I'm going to knee you in the balls while wearing some kind of homemade spikey kneecap thing." I push the image of a hollowed-out porcupine from my mind.

"Just trust me for once in your life, will you?" he says, a trace of a laugh peppering his delicious Scottish accent.

"But I don't trust you." I let my eyes open a tiny bit.

"Don't you dare peek." He shoves his hand over my eyes to stop me cheating. My stomach flutters when I catch the scent of his woody cologne. "Just five more steps."

I count to five and stop. "Are we there?"

His hand tightens on mine and he kisses the top of my head. A swirl of excitement builds over what I'm going to see when I open my eyes. This is just like Christmas when I was a kid. Oh my god, if he's bought me a Polly Pocket Princess Castle Compact, I think I will pass out.

"Okay, you can open your eyes."

What the . . . ? "A drawer."

Ethan's grin spreads wider. "Yup. I tidied it out yesterday. It's yours. You know, for keeping your stuff in. Permanently."

My heart skips a beat. "Wowzers!"

"You like?" His arms circle my waist and he pulls me in for a gigantic hug.

"I do. It looks like I've got myself one of those real-life boyfriend things."

"You certainly have, and yours is pretty spectacular. But this isn't all I have for you." He takes my hand and leads me to the huge, snuggly corner sofa which fills a quarter of his modest-but-manly studio apartment. We both sit, and I pick up on the shift in his mood immediately. His silly, overexcited grin transforms into a more serious smile – but still the most beautiful smile in the world.

"Shouldn't you be getting down on one knee for this?" I say jokily.

He grimaces. "Steady on. I said I was spectacular, not insane."

"Okay, we can save that till our two-month anniversary."

"It's our anniversary?"

Typical. "Yes, a month ago today, remember? You declared your undying love for me outside my flat just as the weather decided to go all monsoon on us."

"It was raining?" he asks with a fake-puzzled expression on his face. I bat his arm and he starts to laugh. "I'm sorry. I do remember the rain. I just prefer to think about what happened after."

Now it's my turn. I make my face go blank. "What happened after . . . when?"

"Very funny," he says, poking his tongue into his cheek in an attempt to stop himself laughing.

I budge up close to him and weave my arm through his. I feel his warmth and the hardness of his body and that gorgeous cologne he always wears, and I can't stop my ovaries from doing a happy dance. This past month with Ethan has been the best month of my life. I feel like I've made it. Like I've finally got what I always wanted, and I'm not just talking about getting my valiant white knight in shining armour, I'm also talking about my great new job. Or am I? Shit, I hope I don't just mean the white-knight stuff because that would be a little 1950s of me. Hmmm. Well, okay, maybe I feel like Ethan *has* rescued me in a way. He chose to love me for who I am, and after a lifetime of not liking who I am, I needed someone to do that. I needed someone to tell me I was special and that I was enough.

"So, come on then. Don't keep me waiting. What's the next big surprise?"

He takes my hands in his, and the hugest, biggest, most beautiful smile spreads across his face like sunshine on the brightest day. "Kenneth Ives."

"Who?"

"Kenneth Ives. I met him last week."

"Who's he?"

Ethan rolls his eyes. "Jeez, Violet. Do you ever pay attention? Kenneth Ives is one half of Lovett Ives, the hugely successful marketing agency that's rolling itself into Tribe – our new agency."

"Ah, okay." Seriously, how am I supposed to remember the names of people I've never met? I have a hard enough time remembering the names of people I have met. I get Facebook friend requests all the bloody time from people I'm sure I don't know, but every single time I click on their profiles I discover I went to school with them or we were on the same course at university. A couple of weeks ago I almost deleted a friend request from Alison Winter, who I worked with for an entire year in New York. She was nice. She looked like Anne Hathaway and she brought me bagels for breakfast.

"You don't know who Kenneth Ives is, do you?"

"Yes, he's one half of Lovett Ives. We've just had this discussion."

"And?" He draws out the word and looks at me as if I've just said I don't know who the prime minister is. I shrug and he rolls his eyes again. "He also owns Helios Villas, one of the UK's most exclusive holiday rentals companies."

How the hell was I supposed to know that? Unlike him, I don't have the *Financial Times* delivered and I don't watch BBC Business Live. "Erm . . . great. Good for Kenneth."

"Violet, you're ruining my very carefully thought-out big reveal here. I expected you'd put two and two together way earlier. Think about it: Kenneth Ives. Helios Villas. We work in advertising. Is anything leaping to mind?"

"No, so could you make whatever it is leap a bit higher? Failing that, you could just bloody tell me."

He twists his mouth and screws up his eyes. "You know, this is actually one of the main reasons I fell in love with you. You're smart, beautiful and incredibly hot, but you're also a complete pain in the arse. I don't even know why I love that so much, but please promise you'll never stop bugging the life out of me. It's such a turn-on."

I lean against him and bring my mouth to his ear. "Are you saying you want to skip my surprise and head for the bedroom?"

He grips my thigh and grits his teeth. "No . . . erm . . . fuck. Okay, I'll make this quick."

He shifts on the sofa next to me and clears his throat. I don't doubt for one second that he's getting a boner, and that thought elicits a drumroll in my lady bits.

"So, as well as being a senior partner in Tribe, Kenneth Ives owns Helios Villas, and although we're still working out of temporary offices and Tribe won't be launching officially for months, Kenneth needs a sixty-second promo, shot on location in . . . wait for it . . ." He takes a deep breath. "Santorini."

A strange, high-pitched squeal leaves my throat. Then I do a double take. Is he teasing me? It would be just like him to do something this mean. Two years ago he convinced Max, our best friend, that he'd be going to the Rocky Mountains to shoot a print ad for Aspen ice cream. When it later transpired that he was really going to the Rocky Mountain Dry-Slope Ski Centre in Slough, Max went apeshit. To make matters a million times worse, he'd already spent hundreds of pounds on a Bogner jacket and a pair of designer ski goggles. "Do you mean Santorini as in Greece, or Santorini as in a Greek takeaway just north of Islington?"

He mockingly brings his hand to his chest. "I'm shocked. You think I'd do something that cruel?"

"Yes, you know you would."

He looks to the ceiling. "Okay, I'll admit I do have form for practical jokes, but this time I'm not joking. Kenneth doesn't own a takeaway, but he does own a travel company and ten luxury villas on Greece's most beautiful and" – he leans in for a kiss – "definitely most romantic island."

His lips touch mine, but for the first time ever, I'm way too excited to kiss him back. "Are you freaking kidding me?"

"See, this still isn't going the way I planned: drawer, Santorini, kiss, sex. It all went so smoothly in my head."

I leap off the sofa and grab my iPhone. "I don't think I have clothes. Or sun cream. I swear, my skin even burns at night in hot countries."

"Are you internet shopping *now*? Do you have to—"

"Wait a minute. Just let me think," I flick onto Selfridges' website and search for bikinis. "Oh, shit. I need hair products. My hair looks wild and unkempt on a normal day, but you should see the state of it when humidity happens. If I don't get the right smoothing serums and de-frizzing spritzes then I'm going to look like a member of Boney M."

"We're not going until Tuesday."

"Tuesday? Tuesday! That isn't enough time." I pick up my bag and head for the door.

"You're leaving?"

"There's too much to do. Three days, Ethan? That's not enough time to plan the ad, and it's definitely not enough time to shop and pack."

"Not enough time to pack? Are you serious? We'll only be there a few days. I thought—"

He looks at me with longing in his eyes, and I suddenly remember the very-near-boner incident from two minutes ago. How the hell did I forget about that? "I'm sorry. You've lost your mojo now, haven't you?"

"You could say that," he says with a chuckle.

"I need to calm down, don't I?"

His smile returns. "You could say that too."

I offer him a weak smile. "Today is Saturday. I suppose I *could* shop tomorrow and we *could* work on the ad on Monday. How's that?"

He stands up, walks towards me and wraps his arms around my waist. “That would be fine, but I’m worried about something.”

I look into his eyes. I can’t tell if he’s being serious. “What is it?”

“You’ve always been the world’s worst procrastinator of everything. You never pay your bills on time. Hell, you have letters lying around for a week before you even open them. We’ve done location shoots before, so why are you getting all jiggly about this one?”

“Jiggly?” I laugh as he gives my nose a cute prod.

“Yes, jiggly. Don’t question my adverbs.”

“That’s not an adverb.”

He sighs in frustration. “Just answer me.”

“I guess I’m just excited. Really excited. Our first holiday.”

“This is work, not a holiday, and we’ve been away before.”

Oh god, he’s not wrong. My excitement level dips when I realise the visions I’ve been having of us sipping cocktails at sunset surrounded by whitewashed buildings will happen with a full film crew and one of our new agency’s senior partners also present. “Well, this is our first trip away for Tribe. And we could still make it romantic,” I say, tightening my grip around his middle.

“This is probably the time to tell you that Max is coming too.”

“Ooh, a threesome.” The words have left my mouth before I have a chance to realise what I’ve said, but I laugh when I see the look of horror on Ethan’s face.

“I hope one day, one hundred years from now, I’ll be able to forget you said that.”

We both laugh and I snuggle against Ethan's shirt. I don't think there'll ever be a time when I don't love how it feels to just wrap my arms around him and breathe him in. We've worked side by side for over three years, but I look at him in a completely different way now. Every time I hear his voice, whether he's arguing with Max over something stupid, talking about a track he's just recorded with his brother's band, or even just teasing the shit out of me, I want to touch him and feel him and hold him. Every time I look at him, my brain screams "I fucking love you", but I wish I could scream it out loud instead of having to keep my feelings secret.

"Violet," he says softly, his faced burrowed in my hair.

"Hmm?"

"I love you."

I look into his eyes and feel a rush of warmth. "I love you too."

He kisses his smile onto my neck, then my jaw, then my lips. He tastes of happiness mixed with excitement. "Bedroom?"

"Absolutely."

2

"YOU KNOW, IN ALL MY thirty-one years of life I don't think I've ever eaten a fig."

"Date," says Ethan.

Max squints in the bright Mediterranean sunshine as he munches on the fruit. "Nineteenth of June."

"What?"

I start to laugh as I realise we're heading headlong into classic Max-gets-it-wrong territory.

"It's the nineteenth of June," he says as he pops another sticky brown fruit into his mouth.

I don't have the energy to explain it to him, and it appears Ethan, reclining on a sun lounger, can't be bothered either. We've been waiting for Kenneth Ives to arrive for the past hour, and I am too hot and uncomfortable. I'm also ungrateful and whiney, because who in their right mind would be unhappy sitting outside a luxurious villa on a beautiful poolside terrace with an actual freaking olive grove in the back garden?

I rummage through my bag and pull out a hairband. My hair feels like it belongs on the back of a camel. I sigh as I scrape the frizzy mess into a ponytail just as an icky river of sweatiness runs down my back. Ugh, why was I so excited to film here? Sun and heat are two of my least favourite things. Along with snow and cold. I realise this makes me the most difficult-to-please person in the entire world when it comes to the weather. I grab my bottle of body mist out of my bag and start spritzing like I've never spritzed

Max coughs, then chokes. "... what the hell is that?"

"Pomegranate and watermelon body ... bottle back in my tote bag.

"It smells like old ladies' underwear."

Ethan looks at him from beneath his ...ni sunglasses and grins. "You know, Max, I'm enjoying today far too much, and the answer to the question could ruin it, but still I can't let this pass. How exactly do you know what old ladies' underwear smells like?"

Max shakes his head wearily. "I have a grandmother. Obviously."

Ethan sits bolt upright and pushes his sunglasses on top of his head. "Max, what do you think I'm going to say next, hmm? It's like you exist solely for my amusement. Why are you the way you are?"

Max shrugs. "Are you telling me your grandmother's knickers didn't smell of perfume?"

"If they did, how the hell would I know?"

Luckily, the conversation is interrupted by the arrival of Kenneth Ives and our Greek film crew. I met Kenneth for the first time earlier this week. He's a leathery-skinned man in his fifties with a huge smile crammed with the biggest, brightest and whitest teeth I've ever seen. As founder and former COO of Lovett Ives, the advertising agency Stella teamed up with to build Tribe, Kenneth used to be a big name in the City. Ethan told me he was instrumental in producing the very first website banner ads in the UK, but for the past decade he's mostly been living in the Med, devoting his time to Helios Villas. With luxury holiday homes in Greece, Spain, France and Italy, Helios Villas features heavily on many a celebrity's Instagram account. And celebrity”, I mean A-list types, not soap or reality show types. He’s the real deal.

Kenneth introduces the Greek crew, all of whom have ridiculously long names comprising a jumble of *K*s and *S*s, which I’m going to have to try very hard to remember and pronounce correctly. Stavros Alexopoulos is a film producer loaned from Vista Worldwide, which is as it sounds – one of the world’s largest multinational ad agencies. Stavros has bright white hair, tanned skin and a rugged square jaw. Ethan pulls him aside immediately to run through our creative brief. Also from Vista are Darius Doukakis, who looks like he’s raided my make-up bag for mascara and eyeliner, and Tony Zorbas, a young guy with a curtain of long caramel hair swinging around his shoulders. Our models for the shoot are Nico Konstantinou, a local actor who I think is a bit too hairy, and Athina Papadelis, who is very beautiful but has even paler skin than me.

We have brunch on the terrace, then Stavros and Darius set up a number of shots at Villa Atlantis, which is the jewel in Helios Villas’ crown. The ten-bedroom holiday rental has spectacular views over Oia, a picture-postcard village carved into a volcanic caldera and painted in brilliant white, cream and sky blue. I’m not going to lie, the setting is more than beautiful, but I don’t seem to be able to take my eyes off Ethan for long enough to fully appreciate it. We’ve only been here one day, but the sun has already bleached gorgeous streaks of gold into his hair, and his body looks amazing in form-fitting navy blue shorts and a loose white shirt. I find a comfy spot in the shade and work on my voiceover script, but every five seconds I break my concentration just so I can look longingly at him.

"How long do you think it'll take for Ethan to bang the Greek goddess?"

Could he be anymore insensitive? He doesn't know Ethan and I are together, but I did admit to having feelings for him. "What makes you ask?"

Max looks at me as if I've lost my mind. "Erm . . . reason one, hot model, and reason two, Ethan."

My blood starts to boil, and I have to order my brain into gear before my mouth leads me to a place I won't be able to return from. "I don't know, Max. It's possible he isn't interested in her."

"Are you kidding me? When has Ethan Fraser not been interested in banging a hot model?"

It's a valid question. And my insides know it's a valid question, hence they've decided to tie themselves up in an angry knot of irrational insecurity. "Maybe he doesn't like her."

His eyes squint into pinholes. "She has two breasts, a vagina and a heartbeat."

For fuck's sake. Just when I'm convinced I have the best boyfriend in the world, Max has to slap me square in the face with a huge dollop of reality. I look over at Ethan and the crew, and my anger turns to rage because of course Ethan would choose this precise moment to adjust the straps on Athina's bikini.

"There you go," says Max triumphantly. "He'll have her out of that bikini and all over his face by the end of today."

"Haven't you got any work to do?"

"Yes, and I'm doing it. I can talk and outline at the same time."

"Well I can't talk and write at the same time, so either be quiet or go away."

Max makes a "humph" sound from the back of his

throat, then he shuffles up his papers and iPad and takes himself over to the cushioned wicker loveseat.

I spend the next couple of hours with my head down, petrified of what my brain will do to me if I see Ethan do or say anything remotely flirtatious in Athina's presence again.

* * *

"Hey, Vi, get your things together," Ethan calls from the poolside. "Kenneth wants a couple of shots at the beach."

My heart plummets to my feet as I look up from my notepad. "Beach?"

Ethan laughs as he walks up the few steps to where I'm sitting. "Yeah, I know. It's a bit of a long shot given there's no sand on a volcanic island, but he still thinks romantic shots of Nico and Athina in the sea would look great. I can't be sure until we get down there, but he's the boss."

A typhoon-level swirl of panic takes hold of me and claws at my throat. "But, you said . . ."

"What is it?" asks Ethan, concern lining his face and giving his voice an edge.

"I . . . I . . . can't."

His eyes search mine. "I don't understand. Talk to me."

I bite down on my lip as my pulse drums in my ears. "You said we'd be shooting here. You said we wouldn't have to leave the villa."

"I know, but Kenneth just came up with the idea. If it's your copy you're worried about, I don't think you'd need to change too much, if anything at all. We're just after a couple of romantic ambiance shots – splashing around in the sea, canoodling on a rock, that kind of thing."

I take a deep breath to try to calm my spiralling emotions. If I'd thought there'd be a chance I'd have to work on a beach, then I'd have taken steps to prepare myself. "I'm sorry, Ethan. It's just . . . ever since Laurel died, I haven't been able to go near the sea."

He pulls out a chair and sits down next to me. "I'm sorry, I'm so dumb. I should have realised." He rests his hand on my knee and gives it a squeeze. "You don't need to go down there, so just stay here."

"I can't stay behind. Kenneth's a senior partner, and our host, and our client. It would look like I don't give a shit about his ad."

He looks at me with so much compassion in his eyes that it's all I can do to stop myself throwing my arms around him. "I could tell him the truth."

"No." I shake my head. "I don't want anybody to know about Laurel or what happened to her. As soon as people know you have baggage like that in your past, they treat you differently." I start gathering up my things. "I'll be fine. I have to be."

* * *

It took over an hour to find the perfect spot. Santorini's rocky coastline lends itself perfectly to romantic scenes, and the small inlet we found has just a tiny amount of pebbled beach, so we aren't overrun by sun-worshipping tourists.

Darius and Tony haul themselves up onto a rock to film from the best possible angle, Nico and Athina try to act as naturally as possible kissing and canoodling in the waves, and Kenneth watches Ethan work with enthusiasm and encouragement. This is where Ethan is always at his best – ensuring his vision makes a smooth transition from brain to camera. In a few months he's going to step into the role of Tribe's creative junior partner. I wonder if he realises this could be his last shot as advertising rock star. A few months from now, other people will be filming award-winning ads while he goes to meetings wearing a suit.

Oh god, my heart. I wish that soul-destroying thought hadn't entered my head. Not for the first time I find myself wishing we could have our old life back. My mind drifts away to memories of when Ethan and I first started working together, then onto the great times we've had over the years. A few months ago we won an AdAg award for Best Advertising Campaign of the Year, and I think I'm yet to process how leaving our old agency and setting up Tribe will be like stepping into a different universe for us. I don't think I'm prepared for the change.

The gentle, rolling hum of the waves crashing against the rocks and the feeling of the sun burning my skin draws me out of that daydream and into another one. Before I know what's happening, it's twelve years ago and I'm back at a different beach – the one that changed my life forever. A dull ache balloons in my chest as I try to stop my mind carrying me away. I try to shut out the sound of her laughter. I try to shut out her calls for help as the sea tore her from me. I try to force the despair, the pain and the grief out of my body and concentrate on the here and now.

I'm not on the beach. I'm not near the sea. I found a secluded space in the shade, far enough away from where they're filming, but close enough that we can see each other. So I'm safe. I remind myself I can swim in a swimming pool so I shouldn't be afraid of the sea anyway. It's been twelve years after all. But fear is hard to reason with – especially when the fear stems from the death of someone whose life gave meaning to mine. I lost Laurel to the sea on a beautiful sunny day in August. That was the day I started to run, and in some ways I still haven't stopped to catch a breath. That was also the day I screamed, cried and wanted to die. It was the day I learned how to hate and the day I became hated, and I'm sure if I live to be ninety the grief will never fully leave me.

I made a promise to the sea that day: *if you give Laurel back to the world, you can have me instead.* Maybe that's why I'm so afraid. Maybe the sea remembers.

"Budge up."

Max nudges my shoulder and jerks me out of my thoughts. I thought he was down at the beach with the rest of them. I move along the bench so he can sit next to me. "Have you put sun cream on your head?" His bald patch has turned a very angry crimson colour.

He pats his forehead. "Yeah, of course I have, but it does feel rather hot. Am I red?"

"You look like a matchstick."

He grimaces. "And you look miserable. What's up? You were weird earlier, and now you're sitting here like Greta Garbo's lonelier, gloomier twin sister."

The only person I've ever told about Laurel is Ethan. I should tell Max, but he gets so protective and emotional at the best of times I'm afraid of how he'd react. At a guess he'd be pissed I haven't told him before, he'd be pissed Ethan knows when he doesn't, he'd be pissed Ethan allowed me to come here . . . the list has so many scary, unpredictable unhinged-Max possibilities that I can't bear to think about telling him.

"I really don't like the heat. Plus, I think I'm hormonal. You know, time of the month—"

"Say no more," he says, eager to stop our conversion heading down a very dark road labelled "woman stuff". Menstruation excuses never fail to terrify the men in my life. "Well, as long as you're okay, I think I'll go for a swim to cool my head."

He pulls his t-shirt off and I start to fear the worst. "Have you brought swimwear with you?" Oh god, please don't let him be planning on skinny-dipping. I couldn't cope.

"I'll be okay in these," he says, referring to his slightly below-the-knee shorts.

"Max, denim isn't great for swimming."

"You think the colour will run?"

"I don't think anybody will be washing their whites in the sea, so you're good, but wet denim is uncomfortable. There might even be some chafing . . . in that region." I point at his groin.

"Oh, do you think I should swim in my underpants?"

"Oh, hell no." I feel my eyes pop. "Max, the last thing the people of this beautiful island want to see is you strutting around in your undercrackers. Go back to the villa and get some swimming shorts, for goodness' sake."

He appears to think about it for a moment, but then he tosses me his t-shirt. "I can't be arsed." And off he goes. I watch him head down the little path to the beach and tiptoe over the pebbles as if they were red-hot coals.

I return to my notepad with a smile on my face, but I still can't concentrate. God, why is my brain torturing me like this? I replay my earlier conversation with Max about Ethan. Under normal circumstances I'd be the first to joke about Ethan's inability to pass a beautiful woman without luring her to his bedroom. We've only been together – secretively and not officially – for just over a month, but all day I've been feeling like a complete fool for thinking his past wouldn't impact on our future. When I watched him with Athina earlier I felt something I didn't like. It was a visceral reaction that went far beyond jealousy. It cut straight down to the bone, making my skin burn and my pulse race. Have I fallen in love with Ethan so hard that I've overlooked all of his fault? As far as I'm aware, he's never hurt anybody whilst enjoying his no-strings-attached lifestyle. Which – again – is more than I can say about my past relationships.

I push all my worries out of my mind as Ethan approaches with his arms full of files and notepads. "Hey," he says with a gorgeous soft tone to his voice.

"Hey."

"So, how are you doing?" He looks over his shoulder to check we aren't being watched, then he reaches for my hand. "I've been thinking about you all afternoon." He gives my hand a squeeze and my fingers lock against his, giving me lovely butterfly feelings.

"I'm okay," I say as his fingers play against mine. Jesus, are we really doing hand sex in public?

"Kenneth has arranged for caterers to serve dinner back at the villa tonight. It'll be fabulous no doubt, but I wish we had some privacy. How about we sneak out once everyone is asleep?" He laughs and the corners of his eyes crinkle.

"We tried that last night, but Max was far too clingy, remember?"

We both laugh. At one point in the evening Max

found a chess board and challenged us to a game. I don't know the rules, so they played while I watched. When all you want to do is take your secret boyfriend to bed and screw his brains out, there is nothing more frustrating.

The crew finish packing up all their equipment and head back to the villa. I break his hold and sigh. "I wish we could be together properly. I know it's selfish of me, and I know I've never been one for sharing how I feel, but for the first time in my life I have something worth sharing with the world." I bring my hand to his face and gently stroke his cheek. "You."

His face lights up with a breathtaking smile as I let my hand fall away. "I know it's hard, but it won't be forever. Stella put a non-fraternisation clause in my contract to protect the agency and to force me to tone down my behaviour. I promise I'll tell her about us once Tribe is up and running and I've earned her trust back."

I know he's right, and although I want to tell the world how much I love him, a big part of me doesn't want our new bosses to think the only reason I have my job is because I'm sleeping with a partner. I'm only twenty-eight, which makes me one of the youngest creative directors in the city. Sure, my portfolio would go some way towards dazzling Saatchi, but with only five years as a copywriter behind me, I'm under qualified as a creative director. Plus, everybody knows I have the people skills of a potato.

"You're right, we have to wait. Tribe is your dream, and you deserve it."

"*You* are my dream, and I wouldn't have achieved a single thing in my life if I didn't have you." He smiles again and my heart melts. "Now let's get our things together and follow the guys back to the villa. We've a couple of hours before dinner, and I plan to spend that time plotting a very hot, but clandestine, after-hours encounter."

"Oh really, who with?" I say teasingly.

He wraps his arm around my shoulders and kisses my forehead. "You. It was always you," he says, taking my hand.

As we walk back towards the villa, I'm suddenly aware of the sea again. The waves crash against the pebbled beach in a rhythm that jars my nerves. I pick up pace, keen to get away, but the feeling intensifies. I stop dead still as the panic spreads from my gut to my chest. "Where's Max?"

Ethan looks back to the beach. "I can't see him now, but the idiot kept swimming into our shot half an hour ago so I told him to get lost. Maybe he's gone back to the villa already."

My pulse races. I start walking back to the beach, my eyes leaping frantically over the waves, desperately trying to spot him. What if he got into trouble like . . . just like Laurel?

"Vi, it's okay. He'll be at the villa irritating the shit out of everybody."

"I would have seen him leave." I feel his hand take hold of mine, his fingers gripping tightly. "He wouldn't have gone back alone, Ethan. I have his t-shirt – he'd have come for it." I try to pull back the panic, but I can't. I must sound like such an idiot. I take a few deep breaths to try to slow my heart rate down.

"I'll call the others." Ethan takes his mobile out of his pocket. "He'll be fine. Just try to relax."

I nod in agreement, but my body is shaking and I don't know how much longer my legs will be able to hold me up. And I feel even worse because I know my out-of-control behaviour is totally irrational, yet I can't stop it.

"Hi, Kenneth, are you back at the villa yet? Um . . . I don't suppose you've seen Max? We seem to have lost him. Okay, give me a ring if you see him."

He ends the call with a grave expression on his face, and my stomach dives into the pits of despair. "I can't bear this, Ethan. I'm sorry. You must think I'm a lunatic—"

He cups his hands around my face and looks at me with so much understanding that my body chokes on a sob. "Hey, don't be silly. This is my fault, I shouldn't have let you come down here." He rubs a stray tear from my cheek with his thumb. "It'll be okay. This is Max we're talking about. He disappears all the time. Remember that conference in Glasgow? He missed the entire thing because he got himself locked inside the hotel housekeeper's storeroom."

I force myself to smile. "God, I was so mad at him that day."

"Me too, but see, he does this all the time. Right now he could literally be anywhere, and I bet he'll have a ridiculous story when he does resurface. I don't believe for one second he got accidentally locked in that storeroom after screwing a hot Romanian maid. It's far more likely he was in there because he was stealing hotel shower gel. He's obsessed with the stuff."

"Ethan, I know you're right, but I can't help feeling . . . and I hate feeling like this. I don't want to feel like this. It's like I'm losing my mind."

He swallows me up in his arms. My head fits in the crook of his neck. His white cotton shirt is slightly damp against his body, and I love how warm he feels.

"It makes total sense that you feel like this, and when I find Max I'm going to kick the shit out of him—"

"What the fuck for?"

I jerk out of Ethan's arms and breathe a huge sigh of relief. Then I do a double take. Max is wearing different shorts, and he seems to have acquired a baseball cap, ugly red-rimmed sunglasses and a double-scoop chocolate ice cream that is rapidly melting all over him.

"Max, where the hell have you been?" yells Ethan.

Max just stares at him open-mouthed. "Shopping."

"You've been shopping? Where the hell are the shops?" he says, mirroring my own thoughts.

"When you told me to fuck off out of your shot earlier, I swam down the coast and found a beach shop. I went back to the villa, changed my shorts, got some money and went shopping." A splat of sludgy brown ice cream lands on his foot. He shakes it off and licks his hand clean of even more drips. "What's the big deal anyway? And more to the point, why were you two hugging?"

We look at each other. Ethan's eyes flash with guilt and my stomach churns.

"What's going on?" Max's tone is laced with suspicion.

"Nothing's going on," says Ethan.

"Bollocks," says Max. He takes another huge lick of his ice cream. "Look at your face. My cat had that exact same expression after he did a poo in my bed."

Ethan's laughs loudly. "Please tell me you found the poo before you went to sleep."

"I was pissed and I was high. I found it all over my face when I woke up the next morning."

Oh god, I'm going to throw up. Made worse by the fact that Max's face is currently smeared from ear to ear with brown ice cream. A torpedo of bile soars into my throat, and it's all I can do to swallow it back down again. "Oh my . . . god . . ."

"Tell me about it. That night marked the last time I ever fed Gunther sardines for his tea." My stomach lurches again and I clasp my hand over my mouth. "But you're changing the subject. Let's go back to you two hugging like you're a couple of lovesick . . . oh no . . ." His face blanches. Even his lobster-red bald patch blanches. "I bloody knew it. I knew this would happen sooner or later. You're banging her, aren't you?"

"No, of course I'm not banging her," says Ethan. "That would be . . . um . . . gross."

What the fuck? Did someone replace my gorgeous boyfriend with an idiot?

"Well, what is it then? And don't lie to me. I know something is going—"

"I was worried about you," I say quickly.

"Eh?" Max screws up his face. "Why?"

I rub my forehead. It's late afternoon, but the sun is still beating down as if it were midday. I don't know if my blossoming headache is due to stress or exposure, but what I do know is I don't want to unleash an outpouring of Max Wolf hysteria into the mix. I can't tell him about Laurel. "I hadn't seen you for ages, and the sea looked rough and . . ." He's looking at me as if he doesn't believe a word I'm saying. "Okay, if you want the truth, here it is. I'm afraid of water."

"Eh? You were swimming in the pool yesterday."

I've always found lying quite easy compared to telling the truth, but clearly my superpowers are starting to wane. "I didn't mean water, I meant the sea."

"Erm, okay. I smell bullshit, but okay."

Ethan steps forward. "It's a phobia, Max. You know,

like the one you say you have about peaches."

"I *do* have a peach phobia," says Max, taking a huge bite out of his waffle cone. "And it has a proper name – fructophobia – and it isn't a laughing matter. In fact, it's debilitating. Navigating the fresh fruit aisle of my local Tesco can be a traumatic experience."

"In case a peach armed with an assault rifle jumps out at you?"

"That's a disablist comment." Max puts his hand on his hip. He takes another, angrier, bite of his ice cream cone. "You wouldn't be laughing if I accidentally touched a peach and went into anaphylactic shock."

"That happens with allergies, Max. There's no risk to your health from an encounter with fuzzy-skinned fruits." Ethan flips his shades over his eyes and picks up my bag for me. "But now you're here, we can all head back to the villa. Kenneth has caterers arriving for dinner at eight. I hope I don't have to tell you to dress smart and don't make a play for the Greek model. She's already told Kenneth that you keep leering at her."

"I do not!" says Max as he follows us up the narrow path that leads back to the villa. "Besides, everyone knows you're the one who'll be making a play for her tonight. You even assigned her the room next to you."

"Firstly, I had nothing to do with assigning bedrooms, and secondly, I don't fancy her. She laughs through her nose and she doesn't speak a word of English."

"Do I need to remind you about Kiki the cleaner?" says Max.

"That was the old Ethan." He nudges my shoulder and gives me a wink. "Junior partner Ethan has changed."

3

KENNETH'S DINNER WAS BEAUTIFUL. I wouldn't be surprised if he'd helicoptered all the best chefs in Greece to Atlantis Villa to cook for us tonight. We were given a choice – kleftiko or grilled lamb souvlaki. I think we all managed to try a bit of both. Well, aside from Athina, who chewed her way through a bowl of salad. I decided she couldn't be happy.

After dinner, we all assemble on the terrace for drinks. The sun is about to set, and the temperature has fallen from "scorching" to "cosy". Darius Doukakis, the bronzed dark-eyed film technician, has brought a guitar to play for us, and Nico, the beardy male model, accompanies him by singing classic Greek folk songs. The music stirs memories of a family holiday to Crete when I was a kid. My parents paid for a "Greek culture evening" which Laurel and I both loved, but this is much better. Max seems to be enjoying it too as his foot is tapping away to the music.

As we all relax, I glance at Ethan, who looks gorgeous in yet another white shirt. I think this might be my new favourite look on him. He meets my gaze and smiles so warmly that I feel a rush of desire deep inside me. I wish we could be alone. After the trauma of this afternoon, all I want is to be cuddled up in his arms. I need to feel his skin against mine and our bodies entwining – and staying entwined – all night long.

Athina takes to the dance floor with Tony, the young

cameraman. Although I absolutely hate to dance, I do like watching other people. Tony claps his hands in the air, stamps his feet, and then twirls Athina around by her waist. They adopt some classic Greek dance moves: arms outstretched across each other's shoulders, legs kicking and side-stepping in perfect unison with Darius's guitar-playing.

"If Ethan doesn't make a move on Athina, I think I will," whispers Max.

I giggle. "Why are you giving Ethan first shot?"

"Because I never get the girl when he's around." I catch a hint of sadness in Max's expression. It's true that Max has never been very successful with women. He dated Tracie Hall, BMG's nerdy data analyst, for a while. She used to spend her lunch hour doing calculus and solving algebra equations for fun, and she came fourth in a national sudoku championship. Max hates maths, so I have no idea what they did when they were together. Then there was the girl who served at the cookie shop near Bank tube station. Max slept with her three times before he discovered her name was "Jae-ni" as opposed to "Jenny". The fact she was Korean should have given him a clue.

Maybe Max is lonely. I certainly know what that feels like, so I try to empathise.

"If you like Athina, you should go for it." I wonder if I'm giving Max false hope. Athina is ridiculously beautiful, and talented, and as we watch her dance, it's clear she's also very confident. I don't think that makes her a cut above Max, or every girl he's ever dated, but *she* might think she is. There's no doubt in my mind that Max would be the most caring, affectionate boyfriend who ever lived, but it's going to take a pretty miraculous woman to see past all of his eccentricities and terrible fashion choices and locate the guy with the huge heart underneath.

"Her English isn't great, is it?"

"Well, no, but it's adequate."

He nods. "Okay, I think I will try. What should I talk about?"

"How do you usually chat up women?"

"Depends. With Tracie I knew she was great at maths, so I pretended I needed some help with my tax return."

"You're on PAYE. You don't do tax returns."

"That's what she said."

Oh dear god. "Max, I think you should just be yourself."

"Well, that's not going to work."

I soften my tone. "Why not?"

"Because . . . well, I don't know. I used to think I had no luck with women because my tallness was intimidating, but that's bollocks, isn't it? Maybe I'm just going for the wrong type of woman. I was attracted to Tracie's super maths brain and Jenny's – sorry, Jae-ni's – super cooking skills. Maybe I should be more like Ethan and bang hot but stupid girls."

Oh, for crying out loud. How the hell do I let that pass? I suck in a huge breath as Max leans in closer to me.

"Will you ask Ethan if he'll let me have a shot with Athina?" he asks.

"I will not!" I suddenly feel a surge of sympathy – and female solidarity – for the poor girl. "She's not a commodity for you and Ethan to take turns with. Jesus! You're swiftly making me lose all respect for you here, Max. What makes you think Athina would be interested in either of you two anyway? Maybe she's a professional woman who takes her career seriously, as opposed to looking to have sex with clients every chance she gets."

He shrugs. "She's a model."

I stare at him open-mouthed. "What the hell is that supposed to mean? Max, you're my best friend, so it's only fair to warn you that you're skating on very thin ice here."

"Okay, okay, why are you being all uptight? She's a beautiful woman. Why aren't I allowed to sleep with her?"

"You are, you're just not allowed to be a misogynistic prick," I say, probably a little too loudly. "Now get out of my sight."

"Fine! Thanks for nothing." He jumps to his feet and struts over to the drinks table to get another bottle of ice-cold Mythos beer.

I shake my head in despair. I'm going to have to sit Max down and have a serious word with him when we get back home. He has his heart set on being Tribe's new studio manager, but Stella already thinks he's an idiot. If she learns he's actually a sexist idiot, then his current zero chance of promotion would fall dramatically to a never-in-a-billion-years chance.

Ethan appears at my left side, drink in hand and a glint of mischief in his eye. "You know, I don't think anybody would miss us if we snuck away."

I glance around the terrace. Kenneth and Stavros are deep in conversation, Darius and Nico are still jamming, Athina and Tony are still dancing, and Max is standing in a corner looking pissed off. Would it look suspicious if we left? Do I even care?

"Where shall we go?"

He jerks his head towards the villa, then turns

around and walks away. I follow him, careful not to make eye contact with anybody as I go. As soon as we're alone, Ethan leads me to the back exit and into the olive grove which covers a small, sloping hillside. The sky has turned a gorgeous shade of indigo, and as we climb the small hill, we only have faint starlight guiding our way, casting eerie shadows in the grass. I shiver and reach for his hand.

"I'm hoping to find a great view at the top of this hill," says Ethan. The grass is coarse, scratching at my feet and ankles. I'm wearing strappy sandals, which aren't an ideal choice for any kind of walking, never mind hill-climbing, but after five minutes we reach the top of the little hill. Ethan sits down on the hard, dry ground and I snuggle in next to him, my insides buzzing with butterflies as his hard body presses against my back.

We sit in silence for a few moments, taking in the view. The villa is beneath us, surrounded by olive trees, and I can make out the path into town that sweeps along the caldera. Oia is painted in shades of blue, with golden lights twinkling from the busy restaurants and bars that will be open long into the night. I look even further into the distance. The sea, dotted with private yachts and cruise ships, is black and still, a strip of silver moonlight leading over the horizon. I think back to my weird freaky behaviour from this afternoon and wonder why I don't have the same feelings about the sea at night that I do during the day.

"What are you thinking about?" Ethan's arm leaves my shoulder and he starts rubbing my back gently.

"About earlier. I'm still a little embarrassed about what happened. I didn't think I'd react so badly. I thought I'd forgotten."

He pulls my hand into his lap with his other arm, forcing me to face him. "I'm not sure people ever forget losing someone they love."

"I wouldn't leave the beach . . . back then." My nose twitches as I sniff back my tears. "I knew she'd gone, but I didn't want to leave. I didn't want to get on the plane. We were there a week, and they took care of her body . . . all the arrangements were made to fly her home. My grandmother, aunts, uncles, our friends – so many people came out to see her. I hated that." Tears fall from my eyes as the memories flood my mind. It's the first time I've talked to anybody about that terrible week. "I hated people seeing her body. I wouldn't see her because I wanted to remember how she was, and if I'd seen her lying there, sleeping, then that image would have taken away my real memories of her. The day we were due to go home, I stayed on the beach for hours watching the waves, feeling the sand, listening to the sounds. I told myself Laurel wasn't in a cold coffin in a cold stone church. She was in the sea, part of the sea, laughing and smiling, telling me she loved me . . . promising that we'd spend a day shopping when we got back home." I wipe at my eyes and rub the wetness from my face. My body shivers. How did it get so cold all of a sudden? "There's a little café in Harrogate that we loved to visit together. It sells the most amazing carrot cake. Laurel used to pour on so much cream that it would run off her plate and across the tablecloth. I've never been back to that café since she died."

"I'm so sorry, Vi. I wish I could make the pain go away."

"It's never going to go away – you were right about that. Grief lasts forever, and losing Laurel is part of who I am. I always thought my grief shaped the worst part of me – the frightened, insecure, self-loathing part – but I don't think that way anymore. I will always love Laurel. I remember how it felt to love her, and I know how to love because of her – that's the best part of me. She isn't here anymore, so I can give that love to you instead."

He inhales sharply at my words as I let my head fall against his shoulder. "I have a lot to thank her for."

I look up into his eyes. "We both do."

"I love you," he says, lifting my chin until my mouth meets his.

I don't think he's ever kissed me so softly or so meaningfully before. He wraps his fingers in my hair and cradles the back of my head. I mirror his actions, moving onto my knees and kissing him forcefully, not able to get enough until our tongues clash together in each other's mouths.

He lowers me onto the grass and we continue kissing each other under the stars. A cool breeze swirls around us. My nipples, pebbled with longing, throb beneath my thin clothing. He stops for a moment and lies on his side, running his fingers tenderly across the goose-pimpled skin of my arm. "How much privacy do you think we have here?" he asks with a laugh.

It's so dark I can barely see the contours of his face, but I know from his tone of voice that he's wearing that huge, roguish smile of his. "I think we're pretty much on our own up here." I sit up and undo three buttons on my dress, letting the straps fall off my shoulders and down my arms.

"Vi, are you . . . serious about doing this?"

I lean forward and kiss him again. "When am I ever *not* serious?" I roll him onto his back and straddle him, feeling his hardness as soon as I lower myself onto his lap.

"Fuck, this is hot." Ethan's fingers grip my hips as I reach behind my back and undo my bra. "I wish I could see you. Why does it have to be so dark?"

"Because it's night and we wouldn't be doing this if it was daytime."

"My wallet is in the villa," he complains as his fingers, then his mouth, find my breasts.

I moan as he takes a nipple into his mouth and pulls hard with his teeth. "We'll have to improvise then." I unbutton his shirt, then I let out a gasp as he rolls my dress and pants down over my hips and grabs my arse, urging me to grind against him. I throw my hair back over my shoulders as I move, hoping and praying that the rustling I can hear in the distance is either a very small animal or the breeze attacking a row of bushes. Shit, what if we're not alone? I can barely see Ethan's face a few inches from mine, never mind what's going on ten feet from us.

Leaves rustle again and I stop dead still, my arms instinctively covering my chest.

"What is it?" His voice is low and intense.

"That noise. Listen."

I lie down next to him, warming myself against his skin. He wraps me up in his arms and kisses me between ragged breaths. "It's just the wind," he says, wriggling out of his shorts and pants. "Stay there though. I like it better like this. I want to feel you close."

His cock rests hard against my stomach as he lays a trail of kisses from my mouth, over my neck and down to my breasts. One of his arms is folded around me, while the other explores my lower body, rubbing lightly on my inner thighs until I open my legs. I need to feel him inside me so badly that I have to resist the urge to skip starters and dive straight into the main course.

As his fingers play inside me, I take hold of his cock and circle the tip with my finger. The contact makes him groan from deep within his throat. “Oh fuck, that feels good.” His cheek is pressed against mine, our bodies are fused together and we’re massaging each other in a rhythm which intensifies as our desire grows.

The skin at the tip of his cock is so taut that it practically squeaks when I rub my thumb over it, and a tiny amount of warm pre-cum leaks from his body. I know he’s close, so I let myself go too. His fingers rub hard on my clit until I come undone. Huge waves of ecstasy ripple through my body. I pull him close and shriek into his neck just as he comes against my hip.

We hold each other tight until our bodies calm.

“Stay with me tonight,” he says, brushing my dampened hair from my face. “I don’t want to sleep alone. I want to talk to you and I want to make love to you . . . but on a comfortable bed.”

“The grass is a bit rough, isn’t it?” I say, knowing the dry ground will probably have etched a pattern into my skin.

He laughs. “Just a bit. I think I’ve got a twig wedged between my arse cheeks.”

“Oh, how romantic.”

“Well, you know, stick aside, this *is* probably the most romantic sexual encounter of my life.”

“Probably?” I ask, batting his arm gently.

“*Probably* until we get back to the villa.” He leans in and kisses me. “When we do this – and more – all over again.”

4

I'M WOKEN OUT OF MY sleep by frantic banging. My back is moulded against Ethan's warm body and his arm is wrapped tightly around me. We both take a moment to rub the sleep from our eyes, then, as the banging gets louder, Ethan sits bolt upright in the bed.

"What the fuck?" he exclaims.

My pulse begins to race. Have we been discovered?

Max's voice booms into our room. "Ethan, if you don't answer this bloody door I'm going to steal your passport and leave you here!"

Oh shit.

"We need to get rid of him." I pull the white cotton sheet around my body. "Fast."

"Are you even in there?" Max shouts from behind the closed door.

Did we lock the door last night? Oh fuck, oh fuck, oh fuck . . . no, we didn't. The doors don't lock. We don't even have any bloody keys.

"I'll go." Ethan gets out of bed, his eyes searching the floor. "Where the hell are my pants?"

More banging. "Breakfast was served half an hour ago and Kenneth is pissed off with you. I don't even know why I care if our new boss thinks you're a liability – you are a bloody liability!"

Ethan picks up a towel and wraps it around his middle. "Calm down, Max. I'll be five minutes."

"Why were you ignoring me?"

"I was asleep. Now go away."

"Go away? I've had to suffer Kenneth Ives wittering on about all the celebrities and millionaires he plays bloody golf with all morning because of you." The door handle creaks, and my stomach leaps into my throat. I pull the sheet over my body, roll over and pull a pillow over my head in the nick of time. Max barges through the door and I pretend to be asleep.

"Max, what the hell? Get out of my fucking room!"

Deadly silence. My heart is beating so hard in my chest that I think it might explode. The pillow I'm holding over my head might be the last thing I ever see.

"I bloody knew it. You never fail, do you?"

"Max, I can explain—"

"Explain what? This is the last time you do this to me, Ethan Fraser. It took me years to forgive you for Yasmin Jones. Remember how much I was into her at UCL? You knew I was into her and you still slept with her. You just can't help yourself, can you?"

My stomach sinks. Oh my god, is he saying what I think he's saying? I've never thought of Max in *that* way and I'm sure he hasn't . . . no, he can't be saying that. I must have misheard. I hope I've misheard. I bury my face so deep in the pillow I can barely breathe.

"Erm . . . Max . . . I didn't . . . what are you talking about?"

"You know fine well what I'm talking about. I told you yesterday that I liked Athina."

Oh my god! He thinks I'm Athina. Of course! Our hair is the same length and colour and that's all he can see of me. I stuff a chunk of pillow in my mouth to stop myself laughing. Then I pray with everything I have that Ethan catches on quicker than usual and doesn't give the game away.

"Okay, right, I'm sorry. We'll talk about it later." I

hear the door creak open, and I exhale with so much relief that I almost choke on the pillow. "Now keep your voice down or you'll wake her."

"I don't give a fuck if I wake her. You're a slut and she's an airhead, just like all the other airheads that end up screwing you. How do you do it, eh? Why can't beautiful women see you're a complete dickhead? I hope you catch syphilis."

"It's not the Renaissance, Max. Now piss off and let me get dressed."

The door closes, but I'm too scared to move. I'm not sure if he's gone.

"Can you believe the nerve of that guy?" says Ethan, and I reckon that's my all-clear. I sit up and hold my head in my hands.

"This isn't good."

"This is worse than no good, this is a fucking shitshow. I can't even remember him saying he liked Athina."

"What do you think he's going to say to her when he sees her this morning?"

His jaw drops to the floor. "Oh shit."

* * *

We get ready as fast as we can. Ethan leaves for the dining room three minutes before I do. I manage to get to my room unseen and swap yesterday's yellow sundress for a short, cornflower-blue one. When I catch up with Ethan, he's sitting at the table, tucking into chilled grapefruit. Darius Doukakis is sitting next to him with a plate of cold meat and cheese. My stomach is still churning too much to eat, so I pour myself a glass of apple juice and take it out onto the terrace.

"Morning, Miss Archer," says Kenneth. I swear his skin has turned an even darker shade of sepia over the last two days. He looks like a prune. "I hope you had a good sleep. We seem to be missing Mr Fraser. I don't suppose you've seen him." I catch Max's sneer at the mention of Ethan's name and dread the inevitable ear-bashing I'm going to get on the flight back to London.

"He's in the dining room. I've just passed him."

Ethan and Darius walk out onto the terrace, followed by Tony and Stavros. I take my drink to the table and sit down opposite Max.

"Ah, here you are at last," Kenneth says to Ethan. His voice has a grain of sternness and disappointment in it. "I was hoping to see you at eight-thirty – like we planned."

"I'm sorry, Kenneth. I slept in."

"Where did you get to last night?"

Max grunts and my insides twist into a knot.

"Erm, when do you mean?"

Kenneth shakes his head. He's flown us all here and given us three days' use of his amazing villa. I don't blame him if he thinks the least we could do is turn up to breakfast on time.

"Okay, we'll talk later. There's something Stavros and I needed to run by you, but because you disappeared last night and slept late this morning, I've missed my chance. I need to go into Oia for an hour or two, so we can talk over lunch – before you leave for the airport. Please be here when I get back."

"I will. I'm sorry, Kenneth."

Kenneth leaves. I glance at Ethan, and he shrugs wearily. Then I see Max glare at him as if he wants to strangle him to death with his bare hands. This is going to be a very long day.

Stavros, whose silver hair is reflecting the sun like a sheet of tinfoil, takes a seat at the table between me and Max. "You disappeared last night too, Violet. Were you with Athina? One minute there was beautiful Greek music and dancing, the next minute I'm alone with Tony, Darius and my new friend Mr Wolf here." He gives Max a playful pat on the back.

"I actually went to bed early, Stavros. I'm not used to this much sun. I had a killer headache."

"Ah, a headache?" says Stavros. His accent is strong and his voice is gravelly. "That's too bad."

"Yeah, it is too bad," growls Max. "If you'd stuck around last night and told *him*" – he glowers at Ethan – "what I told you to tell him, then I wouldn't be in this mood."

"What does this mean?" asks Stavros.

I have no choice but to play along. "Have you got something on your mind, Max?"

Max grunts again. "No, just sitting here processing the fact that my shitty best friend has betrayed me yet again." Everyone falls silent. Max turns the page of his magazine so angrily that he almost rips it. "Where is Athina anyway?"

Darius and Tony talk between themselves in Greek. "She left," says Darius.

Finally, the gods smile down on me.

"When did she leave?" asks Stavros.

"Last night," says Darius.

Oh fuck. The fuckiest of fucks. I glance at Ethan. He looks like he's going to be sick.

"She can't have left last night," says Max, his brow pleated in confusion.

Darius shrugs. "She got a call that her grandmother was very sick in the hospital in Thira, so she rushed to see her. Nico went with her."

It happens in slow motion.

Max's face turns from white to pink to red, then his mouth falls open and his eyes grow to twice their normal size. He leaps out of his chair and points at Ethan, then at me, then at Ethan again, then finally at me again. "It was you! This morning . . . it was you!"

I stand up so quickly that my chair screeches across the tiled floor, making my nerves jar. "It's not what you think, Max."

Darius, Stavros and Tony frown in confusion. Ethan practically runs to my side.

"Yes it is what I think. Don't fucking lie to me you . . . you . . . you liars!"

"Let's talk about this inside." Ethan takes Max's arm and pulls him to his feet.

"No, oh no. I can't. It was you this morning? It was you, wasn't it?" He follows Ethan into the villa like a zombie, his legs shaking beneath him.

As soon as we're inside, Ethan closes the terrace doors, spins around and fixes Max with a glare. "Will you shut up, you bloody idiot?" he says through gritted teeth.

"This is so . . . Oh my god. It's incest!" wails Max.

"Do you know what incest is?" asks Ethan. His eyes are so wide they look like they're about to pop out of his head.

Max walks over to the sofa and collapses in a heap, his long gangly limbs folding around him. He buries his head in his knees. Ethan looks at me in a way that tells me it's my turn to tackle him. I walk over to the sofa and sit down next to him, placing my hand gently on top of his. Surely this can't be that much of a surprise. I admitted I had feelings for Ethan weeks ago. Max even encouraged me to tell Ethan how I felt.

"Max, remember when you told me the mountain wouldn't move if I just sat looking at it?" His head nods twice. "Well, I stopped looking, and I did something."

"Okay." His voice is muffled by his knees. He slowly looks up, his green eyes fixing on mine. I don't think he looks shocked or angry anymore. "I swear to god, if he's made you one of his one-night-stands, I'll kill him."

"Max, it's not like that," I say earnestly.

He glowers at Ethan. "It's always like that with *him*."

"Max, you do know I didn't shag Athina, right?" asks Ethan, one eyebrow raised.

"Yes! I'm not fucking stupid! I know what happened, and I know if you do anything to hurt Violet I'll pay someone to kidnap you and lower your balls into a heavy-duty industrial meat mincer, you got that?"

Ethan's tongue finds the inside of his cheek. "That doesn't sound much fun for me, but I promise this isn't a one-time thing. In fact, we've been together ever since we left BMG."

"Wait. Say again. How long?"

"Over a month."

Max looks between the both of us, and his face slowly begins to soften. "Promise me you won't do anything to hurt her."

"I promise," says Ethan with a shrug.

"No, I mean you have to *promise*. Because if this ends horribly and I have to choose sides, then I'm choosing hers."

Ethan swallows hard. "I promise."

Max gives Ethan a cold, hard stare. "Good. Now . . . I feel better." He pulls me into a hug that knocks the air from my lungs. "Oh my god, I am so happy for you." He releases me and I cough. Christ, I think he crushed my windpipe. "And I'm happy for you too." He stands up walks towards Ethan with his arms outstretched.

Ethan steps back in shock. "Jesus Christ, Max, will you calm down? Nobody can know about us."

"Why?"

"Because Stella will fire me."

"Why?"

"Because she put a clause in my contract stating that she could buy out my partnership if I ever had a personal relationship with a client or employee."

"Why?"

"For Christ's sake, will you stop saying 'why' and just listen!" he yells, then he looks over his shoulder at our colleagues on the terrace and lowers his voice. "Stella was my manager at BMG for almost eight years. She knows me, okay? She gave me a huge opportunity to join her at Tribe, but she doesn't trust me after what happened with Carly and Quest. I can't risk telling her about our relationship until I've earned her trust back."

"And that's why you didn't tell me?"

"We haven't told anyone," I say with barely disguised sadness in my voice. "It isn't a great situation, Max, but sometimes life gives you lemons."

"So you can make lemonade?"

I smile. This could be the first time Max has made sense out of an English phrase. "Something like that."

"Okay, then I will be Mata Hari for you."

"Mata who?" asks Ethan.

Max rolls his eyes. "You know nothing about anything. Mata Hari was the greatest spy who ever lived. I'll keep your secret."

"I think Mata Hari might have been a prostitute,

Max," I say with a giggle. "And an exotic dancer."

"Really? God, I love her even more now. In fact, I've just thought of a plan." He stands up and beckons both of us closer to him. "If you need me to keep secrets or act as a decoy, or plant evidence or something, then I'll do it, but I need a codename. How about 'Maxa Wolfi'?"

"Erm, sure," says Ethan.

"Sounds great to me," I add.

"Great, now we need to pack. I want one last dip in the swimming pool before we go home. These last few days have made me realise I need to take more holidays." He goes off to his room, and I feel the tension float out of my body.

"Well, that could have been a lot worse," I say.

"It could," says Ethan, sweeping an arm around my shoulders. "I wonder how everyone else will react when we tell them."

"*If* we tell them," I say, correcting him.

His brow furrows. "*When*, not if. When the time is right."

5

"ETHAN, WHERE ARE YOU TAKING ME?"

We got back from Santorini two weeks ago, and Ethan promised we'd go out for a special evening when we completed Helios Villa's ad and brochure. He passed the taxi driver a top-secret address, and we've been heading south-west of my flat in Kilburn for the last half an hour.

"God, you're so impatient. Just trust me."

"I've told you before – several times – that I don't trust you."

It's a warm evening in July, and I don't even know if I'm dressed for wherever it is he's taking me. I threw on a knee-length purple sundress with criss-cross straps at the back, thinking a pair of heeled sandals would make the dress look less casual if he was taking me somewhere posh. He's wearing dark jeans and a white shirt – my favourite – but he's clearly gone for a casual look, meaning I've tortured my feet in the heels for nothing.

Two minutes later and we're heading down a familiar street.

"Ethan, is this? Are we . . .?" I look out of the window at the row of neat four-storey Victorian terraced houses and wonder what on earth he's thinking. "You're taking me to your mother's?"

He smiles a huge smile. "I am."

The taxi stops outside Kirsty Cleary's house in Chesilton Road. Ethan pays and thanks the driver, then

I get out of the taxi and stand frozen on the narrow pavement, gazing up at the red-painted front door.

"Why are we here?"

I like Ethan's mum and have met her several times before, but each time she's known me as Ethan's best friend and work partner. I don't relish spending an evening at home with the Clearys pretending I'm not in love with their son and heir. Ethan takes both of my hands in his and gives me a smile that lands a spark of light in his blue eyes. "I love you, Violet Archer, and it's killing me that I have to keep you secret. A few days ago I realised that while I can't come clean about how much I love you at work, I can tell the people who really matter."

His words knock the air from my lungs. "Ethan . . . are you sure? I mean, meeting your mother is kind of a big deal."

His face twists. "You've already met my mother."

"That's not the point."

He laughs. "I know, but I want to tell her about you. And I want to tell my brother and sister. I even want to tell my stepdad – you're one of the few people in the world who he actually likes. They're all here tonight, and they already know I'm bringing my new girlfriend to dinner, so we better not keep them waiting."

"You've told them about me already?" I'm not sure how I feel about this. It's not like Ethan to do something majorly serious without running it by me a dozen times and procrastinating for a month or two.

"I told them I had a girlfriend, but they don't know it's you."

My heart skips a beat and I feel an uncontrollable urge to run away.

He lets out a short laugh. "What's wrong?"

"I . . . um . . . don't know. I think I need longer to prepare for this."

"Don't be silly. My mum loves you, and she's over the moon that I'm finally bringing a girl home."

"You've never brought a girl home?"

"Nope," he says proudly.

"Not even Zoe?" How is this possible?

"No, not even Zoe." He raises his eyes to the sky and gets lost in thought. "Actually, I do remember bringing Mhairi MacKay home for tea once."

"Who?" He's never mentioned that name before.

"Mhairi MacKay. We were deeply in love and one hundred per cent sure we'd get married one day. We were also nine years old. We had fish fingers and baked beans for tea, followed by Neapolitan ice cream with a squirt of chocolate sauce."

I giggle. "Sounds delicious."

"It was. You can't beat fish fingers."

He squeezes my hand tight and opens the gate to his mum's house. I follow him across the tiled yard and up three stone steps. He rings the doorbell and my pulse starts to race.

"You'll be okay," he says as we wait for the door to open.

I clear my throat and nod. My stomach feels like it's inside a washing machine on a spin cycle. *Shit and hell and bollocks, Violet, get a bloody grip for once.*

Thirty seconds later, the door opens and I'm met by Kirsty Cleary's confused, then shocked, then – I think – happy face.

"Oh, my goodness," she says in her gorgeous Scottish accent. "Why didn't I realise Ethan's special someone would be you?" Her small heart-shaped face stretches into a huge smile as she steps to one side.

"Come in, goodness me, come in. Dinner will be an hour."

Ethan ushers me into the house ahead of him, and as soon as I walk into the hallway a small, white, yappy ball of furriness launches itself at me and starts jumping up at my knees. "Oh hi, Angus," I say to the Cleary family's Highland terrier.

"Oh hell." Ethan's hands shoot to his groin. "Mum! You said you'd lock Angus in the basement."

I laugh as I remember the time Angus – arguably the world's most excitable dog – jumped up at Ethan and bit clean through his trousers and underpants. He had to prise the dog's jaws off his family jewels. Ever since that fateful day, Ethan has thoroughly hated Angus.

"Ach, get away with you. He's just a baby."

"He's not a baby, he's a fully grown adult dog and he's also a bloody psychopath."

Kirsty picks up Angus and takes him into a room. When she closes the door Angus whimpers. I feel heartily sorry for him.

"Don't look at me like that," says Ethan. "That dog hates me."

Kirsty Cleary stands in front of us with her hands planted firmly on her hips. "I didn't raise this boy to be frightened of a pup," she says to me, her large blue eyes twinkling with humour. With her slight frame, sharp angular features and fair hair that falls around her face in soft curls, she doesn't look much like her any of her three children, but she is closest to Ethan. They have the same blue eyes, wide smile and lively sense of humour. "Honestly, Ethan, you're the only one in this family who doesn't love Angus."

"That's because I'm the only one he savaged."

At that moment Ethan's brother, who I know well,

appears in the doorway of the drawing room. He leans on the door frame and sinks his hands into the pockets of his jeans. Rory is a musician who also manages a bar in Hackney. He's very good-looking, with thick, dark curly hair that falls to his shoulders, and a neat, hipster beard. He usually wears snug, trendy t-shirts, but tonight he's wearing a checked shirt with the sleeves rolled up to his elbows. Rory shoots me the trademark Fraser smile, which I return eagerly, then he steps forward and gives me a hug.

"Finally," he says when he releases me. "I thought my big bro would never get his act together." He offers Ethan his hand, and the two brothers share a handshake that swiftly turns into another hug. Rory, in contrast to Ethan, is a man of few words, so this is an interesting exchange between them.

We go into the drawing room, where Howard Cleary, Ethan's estate-agent stepdad, is sitting in an armchair reading tonight's copy of the *Evening Standard.* Howard is a large-built, grey-haired man with no neck and a round face. His cheeks look like two shiny apples. "So, I guess I should welcome you to the family, Violet."

"Steady on, Howard," says Ethan. "We've only been dating for six weeks."

"I've known you since you were eleven years old." He strokes his short-bearded chin as he talks. "You wouldn't be bringing a girl into my home if you weren't positive she was the one."

I feel my cheeks heat up, and Ethan's face reddens. I would never have imagined that Howard Cleary, an old-school traditionalist, would be the one who'd make us blush tonight. I sit down on a tan leather sofa and Ethan sits next to me.

"Violet Archer, let me be the first to say that I always thought you were a highly intelligent woman, but now I think you're possibly quite mad!" Ethan's fifteen-year-old half-sister bounds into the room with a serious expression on her face, but a cheeky glint in her eyes. She has thick dark hair like Rory, and a round face like her father, but she's confident and ballsy like Ethan and their mum.

"Oh, why's that, Esme?" I ask, knowing that she's teasing.

"Because my big brother is a big baby who is late for everything, is shit-scared of dogs and forgets about promising to arrange my work experience."

"Watch your language, kiddo," barks Howard from behind the *Evening Standard*.

"Sorry, Dad," says Esme.

"I didn't forget about your work experience. I just don't have much work that would be an experience for you at the moment. Not until Tribe officially launches."

Esme puts her hands on her hips and twists her mouth into a pout. "Fine. I'll go to Dad's office."

"No you won't," says Howard. "Go to your mother's."

"No, uh-uh, I can't. She'll make me bake cupcakes or sell cupcakes and dress up in a pink apron." Esme pulls a face, and I have to agree that the gutsy teenager, with green highlights in her hair and Doc Martens on her feet, would look a bit odd wearing a pink apron. "Rory, can I work at the bar?"

Rory humours her with a smile.

"No, you can't!" Howard's weary voice booms from behind his newspaper.

"Why not?" whines Esme.

"Because you're fifteen years old," says Kirsty,

coming into the room. She's carrying a tray with a floral teapot, jug of milk and bowl of sugar cubes. She places the tray on the coffee table and retrieves six matching teacups from a wooden dresser.

"Grandma's best china?" exclaims Ethan. "You're pushing the boat out, aren't you, Mum?"

"I sure am," she says, pouring out the tea. "It's not every day your son brings a girl home for dinner." She passes me the first cup. I'm not a tea drinker, but I don't want to disappoint her, so I take a sip.

"Rory has brought dozens of girls home," says Ethan.

I glance at Rory, who is still smiling. He gives me a friendly wink.

"Well it's the first time *you* have, Ethan." She pours the last cup of tea for herself then sits down next to me. I turn to face her. "I first met you at Ethan's twenty-sixth birthday party, do you remember?" I nod. Kirsty's cupcake company was starting a new line in birthday cakes, so she threw a party for him, inviting all of his friends. It was a lovely day. "I knew from the way he looked at you that you were very special to him. And then, every time he called me or visited for Sunday lunch, all he ever talked about was you. I knew you'd be perfect for him right from the start."

I expect Ethan to protest at his mum embarrassing him, but he doesn't. Instead, he reaches for my hand, threads his fingers through mine and squeezes tightly. I look into his eyes, and my body is flooded by happy love endorphins.

As I sit in his mum's drawing room, listening to the lively chatter, the warmth from Ethan's touch spreads through my entire body. For the first time since Laurel died, I feel I'm somewhere I belong.

THE END

AVAILABLE NOW

It's Complicated
The Agency – Book Two

Violet Archer has an amazing new job and an amazing man.

She'd be dancing on the ceiling, if she didn't have a pathological hatred of dancing. And if she wasn't terrified of screwing up her first campaign as the creative director of a hot new ad agency. And if she didn't have to keep her relationship with her totally hot best friend, Ethan Fraser, a secret. And if Ethan's list of past conquests didn't read like a Who's Who of the bloody advertising industry.

Violet thought she and Ethan were a rock-solid team. But under the weight of all the secrecy, she feels their relationship – and herself – begin to crumble like a stale croissant. There's no going back to when life was simpler and they had nothing to hide. But can Ethan and Violet find a way forward before it's too late?

Read on for a preview.

IT'S COMPLICATED – FIRST CHAPTER

FUCK . . . FUCKITY FUCKING FUCK.

I lie outstretched on the bed, staring up at Ethan's ice cream–coloured ceiling. Ice cream that's inexplicably melting and running down the walls. "Give me an hour. I'll be okay in an hour."

"Violet, I think that's going to be kind of impossible."

"Why?"

"Well, because you're lying diagonally on my bed, so I can't get in it. Oh, and you're also completely stark bollock naked."

Shit. He's not wrong; I am. "Okay. Forget about the hour. Give me a minute. If I don't barf by the time you count to sixty, I'm still in the game." I squint at him. The zigzag pattern on his shirt draws my brain into a garish, dizzy nightmare, and my stomach turns itself inside out. "Ugh . . . okay, give me two minutes. I'll be fine in two minutes." I crack one eye open to find him grinning at me. "Why have you got clothes on anyway? Are you waiting for a formal invitation to come to bed?"

He runs his hand through his short dark hair, and his grin widens. "We only got back ten seconds ago. I've been in the bathroom having a piss. The most obvious question, given this scenario, is why are you naked?"

"I don't know. It just happened."

He laughs. "Jesus Christ, why did you have to get so wasted? All I've thought about all night is getting you home and shagging you. My cock is very unhappy right now."

"I don't know what you mean. I feel great. Are you

saying I'm not shaggable?"

"Well, you don't look too up for it from where I'm standing," he says, his Scottish accent thick with a mix of humour and disappointment. "Aside from your choice of clothing, that is." He walks over to the bed and sits down next to me, nudging my outstretched arm.

"Stop. Don't touch me. Don't make me move." A wave of nausea rises into my throat and I clasp my hand to my mouth. "I swear if you come any closer, I'll puke all over you."

"Not the most enticing invitation I've ever had." He gets off the bed and disappears around the bend of his L-shaped open-plan studio apartment and into the kitchen area. I use the time alone wisely. I concentrate hard on taking deep, medicinal breaths. *In, out. In, out. In, out.* Wait, why am I having to concentrate so hard on remembering how to breathe? That's stupid. I open my mouth and attempt to suck in a huge lungful of air, but a Chardonnay-flavoured burp zooms up from my stomach at the exact same time. I inhale the burp instead. Gross. I turn over, cooling my face against the crisp cotton duvet. I practise inhaling and exhaling sideways instead.

"Here you go, Sleeping Beauty." Ethan plonks a bucket on the floor, places a pint glass of iced water on the side table and shoves a bubble-pack of paracetamol into my hand. "You need to rehydrate. You must have drunk two bottles of wine by your-bloody-self tonight."

I groan as he offers me his hand and helps me to sit. "Correction: two bottles of wine, two vodka cocktails and an electric-blue shot of something horrible that Max gave me." I feel dreadful, but he looks impressed at my alcohol roll-call. I pop out two pills and reach for the water, taking a succession of thirsty gulps until the glass is empty.

"Jesus, Vi. For such a small person you can't half drink."

I hiccup, and a few drops of water escape out the side of my mouth and land on my bare chest. Ethan watches as I rub my hands over my boobs to dry them.

"Any chance you could accidentally spill some more water and let me do that?" he says, his eyes bright with longing.

I giggle and wrap my arms around his neck. "If I didn't know better, I'd think you let me get in this state on purpose."

His hands move to my waist and he leans in to kiss me. "Now, why would I do that?" he asks, a soft groan escaping his throat.

I brush a trail of soft kisses down his neck, then whisper into his ear. "Because when I'm like this, you know I'll let you do anything you want to me."

"Oh my fucking god, it must be my birthday."

I stand up and position myself between his legs. A swell of desire builds in the pit of my stomach. For a second I forget that I can't see straight or stand vertically without lurching like a newborn foal on roller skates. Could I be any less sexy? Probably not, but there's still something about consuming a vineyard full of wine that makes you believe you have the sex skills of a porn star with debts to pay. He's fully clothed, I'm not, and I can see from the ravenous look in his eyes, combined with the discernible bulge in his pants, that that fact is making him as horny as hell.

I push him back on the bed, kneel between his legs and start grappling with shirt buttons that won't open and a belt that refuses to budge. I force my eyes to work, but the ridiculously small golden buttons must have been sewn onto his shirt by Rumpelstiltskin's wicked stepmother. Did he even have a stepmother? Oh, who cares? I try to forget the room-spin and focus on the task at hand, but I soon get lost in a psychedelic kaleidoscope of pulsating blue zigzags that are now glowing, jiggling and blurring against the liquefied ice-cream walls. Not only has the room been designed to make me puke everything I've eaten and drunk today but it also wants me to hurl my stomach, liver and large intestine up too.

I try to hold it all back by sheer willpower, but when the bed starts spinning off the earth my insides heave.

"Vi? Oh fuck. Get that bloody bucket now!"

He shoves me up and I drop to the floor with a clatter, landing on my knees with excellent timing. I hunch over the bucket, and my stomach promptly expels all that seemed good earlier in the evening. I hate being sick. It has to be the worst, most out-of-control feeling in the world. My skin, suddenly aware of the October chill, is hot and cold at the same time. I barf up the last remaining chunks of my pan-fried scallops, then I let out a sob as my outer head bangs angrily against my inner head. "I think I'm going to die."

He hunkers down next to me and cuddles me into his chest. "You're not going to die, but I might. Did you know cock-blocks could be fatal?" My body checks my stomach is evacuated by forcing me to dry-heave up oxygen. I feel disgusting and stupid, but he just wraps his arms back around me and smooths my hair from my face.

"You think you're done?" he asks, and I nod. I know I don't deserve him. How can he still love me when I look and smell like I've been dragged out of a wino's dustbin? He reaches over to pick a t-shirt off his bedroom floor and helps me put it on. "Sorry, this isn't clean. I'll get you something from your drawer in a minute."

"Given I stink of regurgitated seafood, I wouldn't worry about that," I say. He laughs and pulls me close to him as we sit on the floor, our backs resting against the bed. "I'm sorry. I was just so happy you won the Belle Oaks account. I got a bit carried away."

"Ya reckon?" A flash of lamplight catches the silver in his blue eyes, and my heart flutters. His eyes are my favourite thing about him.

"Was I a disgrace?"

He takes my hand and gives it a squeeze. "No, you were funny, and gorgeous, and totally, wonderfully, amazingly captivating."

I smile as I think back to the evening. I always dread work dos. Making myself interesting to people, and interested *in* people, is not my area of expertise. It comes effortlessly to Ethan, but not so to me – Miss Overthinker of everything. I spend so much time worrying I'll say the wrong thing and look stupid that I end up saying nothing at all. That's how I got into this mess. I was seeking false confidence from Belle Oaks's unlimited supply of free celebratory wine.

I snuggle closer to Ethan, trying to ignore the smell of scallops and wine that's still coming off me in waves. "Hey, now that Belle Oaks is our client, do you think I could get a discount? I love her handbags. I have two already, but they cost the best part of a month's salary."

"Don't ask me. I always thought Belle Oaks was just the name of a shop. I'm still a bit weirded-out that she's a real-life living and breathing person. All last week I half expected Stella to tell me she'd arranged a meeting for me with Dorothy Perkins."

"Well," I say, yawning. "I'm really excited to work on Belle's campaign."

"You should be excited. It's your first job as creative director."

I smile at the mention of my new and extremely important job title. "And it's the first client you've signed up as managing partner."

He grins. "I still can't believe I won it. It helped that Belle is Stella's mate from way back, of course, but jeez, it was a tough sales pitch. The woman's a dragon. She definitely signed up to the Stella Judd School of Ball-Breaking Badassery."

"Oh god, that's the part that scares me. I'm going to have to work closely with her. I'm bound to make a fool of myself. Stella thinks I'm an idiot, so she will too." I shuffle onto my knees, pulling down the hem of Ethan's snug-fit Kasabian t-shirt in a vague attempt to cover my arse.

"Stella doesn't think you're an idiot, and you'll be fine with Belle as long as you remember to flatter her. You like her bags, so you're halfway there."

I try to stand up. "Ugh . . . I am going to die. If I don't see tomorrow, you're my sole beneficiary. Except for my books. Max can have my books."

"He can have your music too. There's no place for opera and show tunes in my life."

"Fine." I'd usually protest my superior musical taste, but I don't have the energy.

Ethan helps me crawl into bed, then he tucks the duvet around me and kisses my clammy cheek. "I love you," he says.

"I love you too."

* * *

Sleep is broken by a familiar "ping", followed by an irritating tip-tapping sound.

I slowly peel one eye open and I'm blinded by sunlight. My brain whirrs, then cracks as I remember that today is Wednesday, I have a ten-hour workday ahead of me and I must have seen every hour of the night whilst either on the loo or groaning in self-inflicted agony.

I stir slowly, craning my neck to peek at the clock – 6 a.m. – thank Christ for that. At least we haven't overslept.

Ping.

"Is that you or me?" I ask, scanning the room to see where I flung my iPhone last night.

"Morning, beautiful." Ethan bends down and gently plants a kiss on my forehead. I don't blame him for steering clear of my lips. My mouth tastes like I've been gargling with rotten eggs and dog shit.

I watch him type, then reality hits. "Ethan, is that my bloody phone?"

"Yeah," he says, giggling. "Max texted you last night."

My weary, poisoned-by-alcohol stomach falls flat. "Oh, no. What have you done?"

"Shush. Don't interrupt me. I'm trying to save your skin. Max is pissed off you left early last night. He wanted you to help him woo Belle Oaks's assistant – you know, the pretty French girl with the cute freckles and the . . ."

I shoot him a glare and he promptly shuts up. We're coming up to our five-month dating anniversary, which follows three of the absolute best years of strictly platonic friendship. He knows I know there's a good chance the cute French assistant would be lying on my side of the bed this morning if present-day Ethan was swapped for five-months-ago Ethan.

"She was called Emily, right?"

He clears his throat and affects a French accent. "Amélie."

"Ah, very Audrey Tautou. Poor Max."

"What do you mean 'poor Max?'"

I prop myself up on one elbow. "I love him. We both love him. But he's punching above his weight a little bit, isn't he? She's kind of ridiculously beautiful . . . and perfect . . . and young . . . and sane."

He raises his eyebrows. "You'd have gone for my throat if I'd said something like that."

"True, but I'm saying this with kindness. I don't want him to get hurt." I force myself to sit up, find the packet of paracetamol from last night and pop out another two pills. "I am never drinking again."

"Hmm?" he says, continuing to type.

"Ethan, what the hell are you texting?"

"You mean what are *you* texting? He thinks I'm you."

"Oh no, don't you dare. The last time you got your hands on my technology you arranged a date for me with Daniel Noble."

"Don't worry. Trust me." He finishes what he's typing then settles down in the bed. "He sent you six messages last night. The first one . . . Here it is . . . '*Where the hell have you gone? Is Ethan with you? If he is, tell him I'm pissed off and I've killed both of you five times over in my head. You're a pair of bastards.*'" Ethan laughs, but my blood pressure is already raised. "That pinged through at two a.m. when you were dead to the world, so see why I had to reply? You made Max lose his shit, and you know what happens when Max loses his shit." He makes his balled-up fists "explode" and says, "Boom!"

And I know precisely what he means. It isn't unusual for Max to need days to crash back down to earth after he's got himself wound up over something. He didn't speak to us for three days last year because we selected Penny Piper's illustrations for a bran cereal promo instead of his. He'd convinced himself we'd done it to teach him a lesson for missing a deadline.

Ping.

I snatch my phone out of his hands and find the new message. I click on Max's name, and it's as I feared. "Oh shit, he's texting me in all caps. Well, half of it is in all caps; he must have realised he was shouting part way through . . . Oh, what the hell? Why is he so angry with me?"

"Because you gave him *really* bad advice, you dipshit."

"Ethan, I swear to any god who will listen, if I have to spend all day fixing an epic Max-sized clusterfuck you created, I'm going to bitch-slap you into next week."

He winces and narrows his eyes. "Have you ever considered changing your name to Violent?"

"Ooh, I like it. Violent Violet would be a really cool supervillain name, wouldn't it?"

"It would be a shit name. Violent Violet sounds like she's been created by Roald Dahl. She might be able to knock out Willy Wonka, but Batman would kick the crap out of her."

I don't bother engaging. I'm too pissed off with him. I stare at the text message, shaking my head: *WHERE THE FUCK ARE YOU? I KNOW YOU'RE NOT AT*

HOME. I SWEAR IF YOU'RE WITH HIM I'M GOING TO HUNT YOU DOWN AND KILL YOU. I SUPPOSE YOU THINK ME WASTING A FORTune on a room at the fucking Birch Royal is funny? I know this is down to him. Tell him he's a piece of shit and tell him to fuck off. All the way off – to hell and back again! Actually no, not to fucking hell and back again. A one-way ticket to hell! I hope he fucking stays in hell. With the devil's pitchfork sticking right up his fucking arse.

Given that English is Max's second language, I've been impressed by his creative use of expletives for quite some time, but here he surpasses himself. Is he trying to win a "how many fucks can you place in a text message" award?

I slump back on the pillows. "Just tell me what you did."

"Okay, but it isn't that bad. I just told him to book a room at a five-star hotel then make sure he got to escort Amélie home safely in a cab. The plan was to slip her the hotel address and room number once he's halfway there."

"What the hell were you thinking? You made Max into a creepy stalker. She'll have him for sexual harassment!"

A fleeting worried look crawls across his face, but then he shakes his head. "Well, it should have worked. This very same move was tried and tested by me with Erin from Sunta Motors two years ago." I roll my eyes at him, but he continues. "Anyway, Max thinks you sent him the tip. You told him a London Symphony Orchestra cellist called Dirk took you to the Ritz for a steamy night of passion."

"What the actual hell? Max is going to think I'm an even sluttier version of you! You could have at least given me a hot-sounding made-up fuck buddy. Why would I have a one-night stand with a stranger called Dirk? I actually feel sick at the thought. Dirk is making me feel sick. If I had anything left in my stomach right now, you'd be wearing it."

"You're saying that now, but you weren't when Dirk brought out the massage oils and handcuffs."

My jaw drops. "Ethan, this is serious. Max is going to hate me for this. And think I'm a slut."

"Leave it to me, I'll set him straight. I'm great at sweet-talking him. All it takes is a bottle of that weird fruity beer he likes. He's like a puppy after you throw him a bone – friends for life."

I climb out of bed and walk over to Ethan's huge wall-length closet. I take out a dress, then retrieve my make-up bag and bundle of toiletries from the drawer he gave me. This drawer is the only tangible evidence of our relationship. I was so happy when Ethan gave me my drawer, but recently I've found myself yearning for more.

"What's the matter?" he asks, catching me lost in thought. He gets out of bed and walks around to where I'm standing. "Look, I'm sorry about Max. I promise I'll set him straight, but I was trying to get him laid. It's been a while for the poor bastard."

I close my drawer and let out a sigh. "Max has been great about us being together, and he's the only person who knows. This isn't a good way to repay him." I try, but totally fail, to stop a note of bitterness creeping into my tone at the reminder that I can't share my happiness with anyone else.

"Hey, I know it's tough. I want nothing more than to tell the world how I feel about you too, but you know the score – no work relationships. Stella put that clause in my partnership contract because of my past, and I need to earn her trust back. My getting involved with a client played a huge part in BMG losing the Quest account. I promised you I'd work on Stella when the time's right, but that time isn't now. Tribe hasn't even launched, so I daren't approach her yet. I know it's hard, but please . . . just a little longer."

I force a smile. "I'm sorry, I'm being selfish. I just can't help thinking back to the summer, in Santorini. We had a great time doing that impromptu campaign for Kenneth Ives. I wish we could go back to how we were then."

He lets his thumb smooth over my jaw as one hand moves to softly touch my hair. "What matters is *we* know we're together. I've wanted to be with you for so long, and I'm so sorry I can't make it perfect for you. This isn't the way I want things either, but the most important thing is we love each other, isn't it?"

I nod. After spending my entire life believing I was unlovable, the fact that I have the most amazing boyfriend in the world is all the perfect I need.

It's Complicated is available to buy as an ebook or paperback from 3rd April 2018.

A WORD FROM GUNTHER
(Max's cat).

If you enjoyed this book, then *purr-lease* would you consider leaving a positive review on Amazon?

Reviews help other readers find Elizabeth's stories and open up different ways of marketing to all the millions of humans out there who will love her books.

She says I (or rather my idiot owner) might get my own story if I can *purr-suade* you. I personally don't know how this will work. Max is a liability. He still hasn't realised that I'm the one who steals the Serrano ham out of the fridge. I've been doing it for seven years! Seven!

Mee-ow

Do you like free books?

Always You – a short story prequel from Ethan's POV – is available for FREE from all leading online retailers.

How it all began . . . Just Friends is the first book in the Agency series.

WHAT'S NEXT?

The Agency Book 3
2019

ABOUT THE AUTHOR

Elizabeth Grey spent a sizable chunk of her childhood in North East England locked away in her bedroom creating characters and writing stories. Isn't that how all writers start?

Following a five year university education that combined such wide-ranging subjects as fine art, administration, law, economics, graphic design and French, Elizabeth entered the business world as a marketing assistant before moving into operations management.

Marrying Chris in 2007, Elizabeth now has three young children and runs a small, seasonal business selling imported European children's toys and goods. She is active in local politics and campaigns tirelessly to improve the UK's education system.

During her time as a stay-at-home mum, Elizabeth rekindled her love of writing and thinks herself lucky every day that she is now able to write full time.

When not working, Elizabeth finds herself immersed in her kids' hobbies and has acquired an impressive knowledge of Harry Potter (thanks to the big boy), Star Wars (thanks to the little boy) and Barbie (thanks to her daughter). She loves European road-trips, binge-watching Netflix series and doing whatever she can to fight for a better world.

She's been told she never loses an argument.

Elizabeth's favourite quotes:

"*Real courage is when you know you're licked before you begin, but you begin anyway and see it through no matter what. You rarely win, but sometimes you do.*" – Harper Lee

"*In this life, people will love you and people will hate you and none of that will have anything to do with you.*" – Abraham Hicks

"*Be who you are and say what you feel. Because those who mind don't matter, and those who matter don't mind.*" – Dr. Seuss

"*I am no bird and no net ensnares me. I am a free human being with an independent will.*" – Charlotte Bronte

"*I am not afraid of storms for I am learning how to sail my ship.*" – Louisa M. Alcott

Printed in Great Britain
by Amazon

60478665R00045